ERGO

To Lara – A.D.

To all the children asking their
first big questions – V.S.

First published in 2021 by Walker Books Ltd, 87 Vauxhall Walk, London SE11 5HJ

This edition published 2022

2 4 6 8 10 9 7 5 3 1

Text © 2021 Alexis Deacon • Illustrations © 2021 Viviane Schwarz

The right of Alexis Deacon and Viviane Schwarz to be identified as author and illustrator respectively of
this work has been asserted in accordance with the Copyright, Designs and Patents Act 1988

This book has been typeset in Helvetica Neue

Printed in China

British Library Cataloguing in Publication Data: a catalogue record for this book is available from the British Library

ISBN 978-1-5295-0418-7

www.walker.co.uk

Ergo

Alexis Deacon illustrated by Viviane Schwarz

WALKER BOOKS
AND SUBSIDIARIES
LONDON · BOSTON · SYDNEY · AUCKLAND

Ergo woke up

and set off to explore

the world.

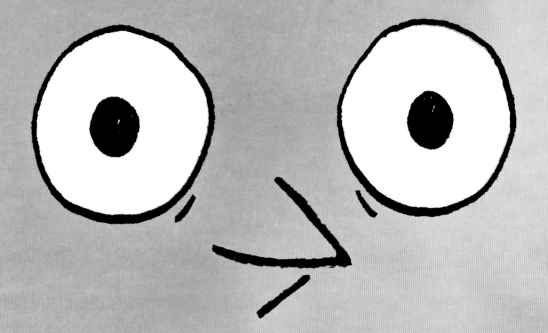

The first thing she found
were her toes. They wiggled.
Wiggle, wiggle, wiggle.

WOW.
GREAT START,
she thought.

She decided to keep on exploring.

She found her wings. Flap, flap, flap.
She found her beak. Peck, peck, peck.

And she found her legs. Kick, kick, kick.
That was all she could find.

AM I THE WORLD?
thought Ergo.

It was a small world.

She wiggled her toes, she flapped her wings,
she pecked her beak, she kicked her legs.

She was happy,

I AM THE WORLD AND THE WORLD IS ME,

she thought.

I FOUND EVERYTHING!

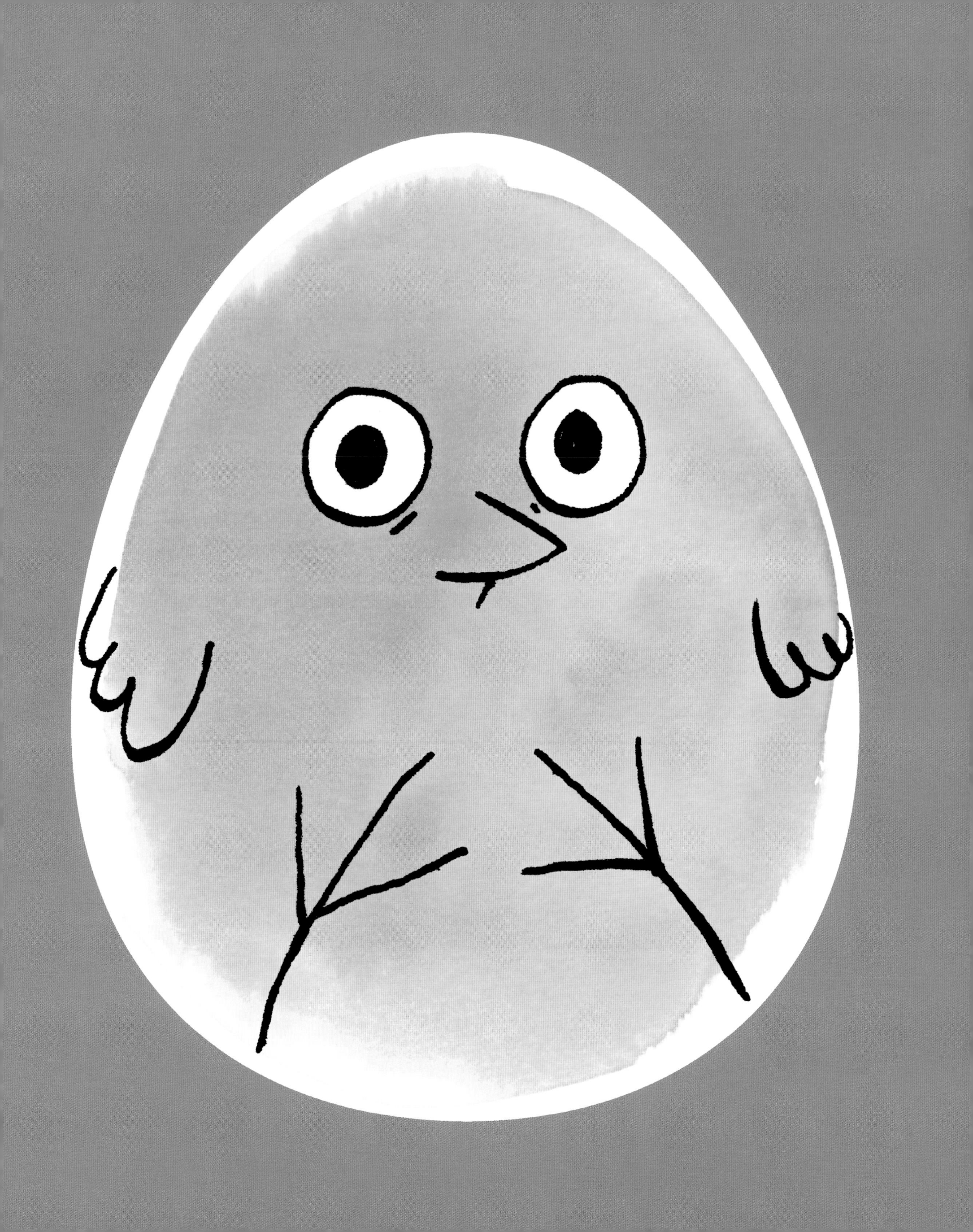

Then she saw the wall.

IS THAT
ANOTHER
PART OF ME?
she thought.

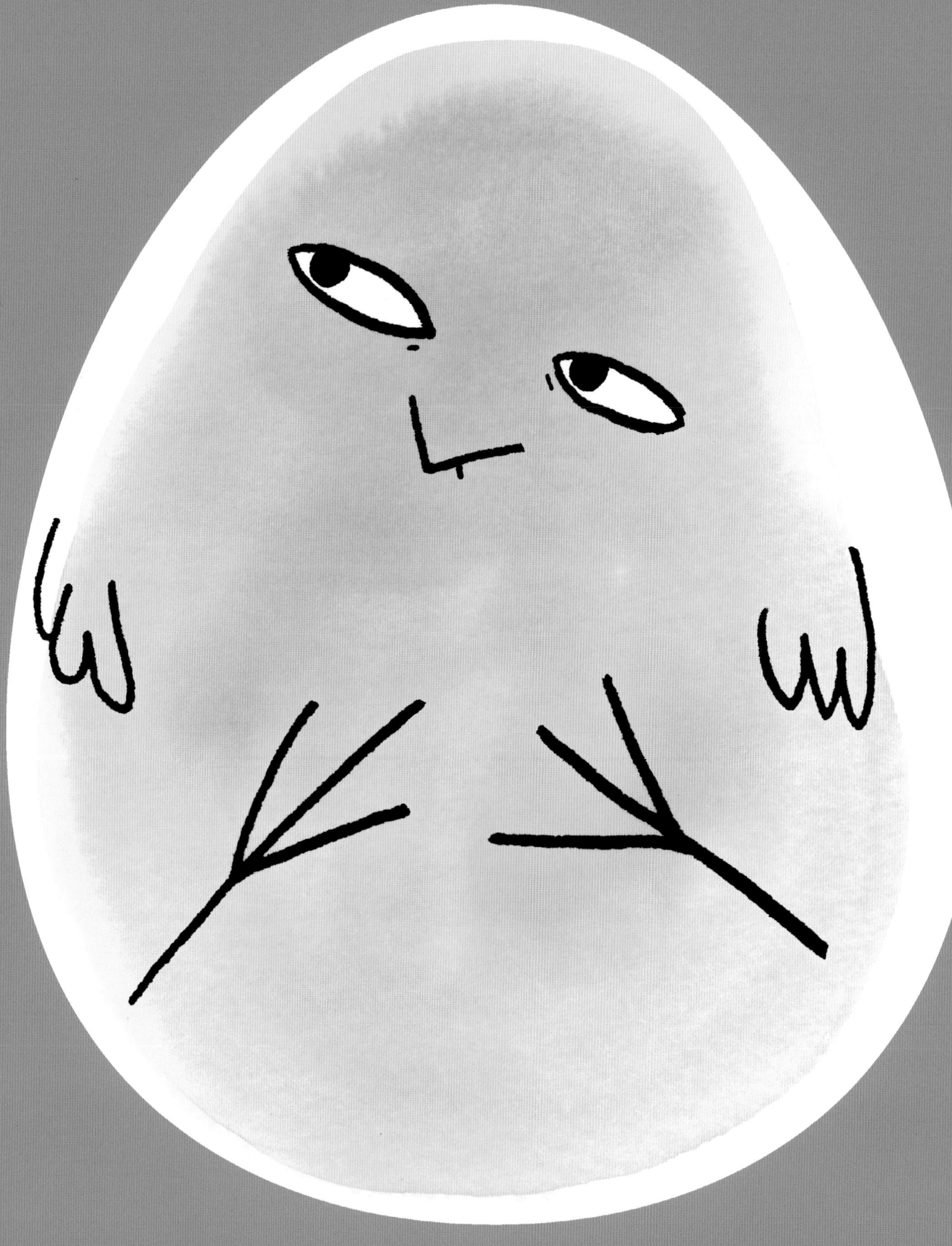

She pushed the wall.

And her whole world
rolled round and
round and round
and upside down.

I CAN MOVE THE WORLD,

she thought.

It was a big thought.

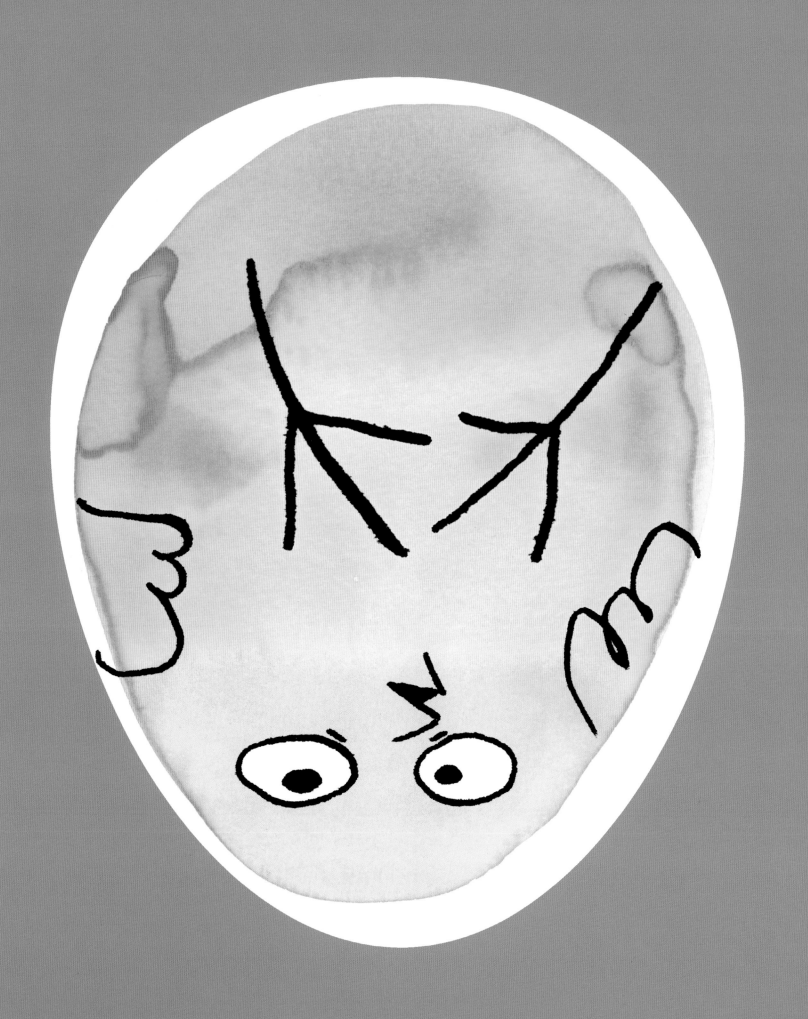

Then something went

BUMP!

THAT WAS NOT ME.

THAT WAS SOMETHING ELSE!
thought Ergo.

I AM NOT THE WORLD,
thought Ergo.

But what else could there be?

She tried to think but all
she could see were toes wiggling,
wings flapping, beaks pecking
and legs kicking.

She tried to fit them
all together. But it
was no good.

NOT KNOWING

IS NOT GOOD,

thought Ergo.

STICK TO WHAT YOU KNOW, thought Ergo. She imagined other worlds exactly like her own.

WHAT IF WE ARE ALL STUCK INSIDE WALLS, ALL SCARED OF EACH OTHER, NEVER KNOWING WE ARE JUST THE SAME?

Ergo looked at her wall.
THE TRUTH IS ON THE OTHER SIDE,
she thought.

She wiggled her toes, she flapped her wings, she kicked her legs and pecked her beak as hard as she could.

And all around her came the same sound

Louder and louder until…

CRACK!

Ergo's life began.